A Ghost Story

By  T Y Scott

ISBN 978-0-6151-8428-9

I'm starting this book by saying that this is a ghost story above all the other things that It might seem to be. I do not want to confuse people. Any link to anyone or any place is just a coincidence and that is all. It Is not based on any one person. Just myself. Now I ask you, do you believe in ghosts? I do.

Chapter 1

The morning

The day I was born was not the happiest of all days . The birth of a baby should always be happy, but for me it was a day of deep and utter grief. My parents, while on the way to the hospital, where hit by a drunk driver . The doctors removed me from my mothers dead body . I was not greeted into this world by a loving father or mother, there was no pink balloons announcing that I was a baby girl loved by her family. This began my close relationship with death. From the time of my birth I was shifted from foster home to foster home. No one really seemed to want to keep me for long . They said I was rather odd and not like the other kids. So by the time I was ten I had been in Thirty eight homes when I landed in the home of a woman named Beth. Beth was a kind woman. She never yelled, not even from room to room like most people do. We became close. I was the only foster child she had so I guess when you're all alone in a house together that kind of thing happens. The school I went to was like all the rest. When the kids find out you are a foster they tend to think something is wrong with you, so they stay away. That's not to say I didn't have one friend, 'cause I did , his name was Jim. We would play after school at my house and sometimes his mom would let him stay for supper . When I turned eleven Beth gave me a party. I had never had a party before or even gone to one for that matter. None of my classmates came but Jim. Me and Jim were so close  it was just natural that when I turned fifth teen Jim wanted to be my

boyfriend. So, I said yes. We grew closer with time so that after graduating from high

school we were married. Jim got a job at the local shopping center in town and I started

fixing up an old house that I received in my parent's will when I turned eighteen. It was

odd being in the house . The lawyer over my parents will met with me and my husband

to give us the keys and show us around. What I have to say that upset me more then

anything was not the pictures of a family I had never gotten to know but was the room

that was going to be mine. All the baby clothing, and all the other things set up waiting

for a baby that never came home.

The first few months was hard for us, living on our own and all. But we got through

things together as any couple does. One day, as I was cleaning up the supper dishes , Jim

came to me and asked me if I had been to the attic yet to see what was up there. When I

replied no he suggested that we should do that. The next day was a Saturday so we went

up to the attic to check it out.

Chapter 2

The Discovery


The attic was larger than what I expected. It was full of different things; from old

clothing to painted pictures of people I had never seen before. I have to admit I was very

surprised and happy about it all. I never had a real link to my family before and living in

what was once their house , even though it was a comfort sometimes, at other times it

seemed almost morbid. While looking around through old papers we found out that my

family owned another house about an hour or so from this one. This was shocking cause

the man over my families' will never told us about it. So maybe he didn't know it either.

After talking about it for a little while we decided to go and have a look at the place for

ourselves. We loaded up into the car  and headed out. The day was so pretty I remember

thinking about how nice it would be to stop at the beach on the way back home and

watch the sun set. I always did love sun sets. Seeing the way the sun moved down

toward the earth making the sky change color . It wasn't very long before we were

turning into the driveway of a long empty home. It was a very large with four stories and

porches going all around each of them. It resembled an old plantation home I had seen

in a book once. I remember feeling a chill standing there looking at it , like it was

looking at me to. Sizing me up like I was sizing it up. Watching me, waiting to suck me

into  it.

"Hey, are you ok", It was Jim, speaking to me, but all I could do was look at this house.

"Yeah, I'm ok. It's just that it is so big!"

"Well, big is good. It looks like it might need some fixing up though".

"Fixing up for what?"

"To sell".

"No… we are not selling this house, not now, not ever!"

I could not breathe. Just standing there in front of this monster of a house I could not breath. Not wanting to go into it and not wanting to get rid of it either. The breath had left my body and was not coming back to it. It was getting dark, I felt myself falling backward seeing the sky coming down into view, then, nothing but blackness. O god ,was I dead?… was this the death that had finally found me after all these years? Had it come for me today the way I had always wished it would? Then I saw him, a strange man with blond hair and pale blue eyes. He was there beside me, I turned to look at him, I reached out to him, for him to take me wherever he wanted me to go. Then ..he was gone! I heard Jim call out to me, it was all over. I opened my eyes, not in death but to life. I had passed out, that was all, just fell over. As I sat there on the ground I could not help but think about the man I had just seen. Who was he? Why did I see him? Looking at the house before me I knew the only way to find out was to go inside.

# Chapter3

## The house

We found the key under an old faded flower pot on the front of the first level porch.

It was a little hard  unlocking the door. It seemed to have been a long time since anyone

had been in the house. When we opened the door our senses was automatically assaulted

by the stench of stale air ,rot, and something that I could not really place, but I was sure

I did not really want to know. We entered into what looked like a scene from a scary

movie. You know, the one  where the unsuspecting  couple enter into the old house and

a mad man is hiding in the house to kill them. Yeah , I felt that way, like there was

someone there already watching us, waiting for the right moment to jump out and kill

us. But still we walked forward into the dusty old house like we were willing fate to take

over.  To the credit of the house, it was not so bad. A little cleaning up, some paint and

you could live in it . Of course, there was all the cobwebs and spiders to deal with but

that was life. The room in which we had entered from the doorway  was rather large ,

with a staircase leading up on both sides of the walls. In the center of the room was what

at one time had been  a large flower pot, but now was filled with dead brush. There were

rooms to the left and right of us.  We picked the right one and started to explore the house. The room on the right lead into a large dining room that had a table that would seat at least forty people easily . On the table there were two place settings, one at each end. In the middle of the table was a beautiful candle holder. On the walls around the room were pictures that we recognized from the paintings we found in my parent's house. We walked the length of the room moving toward the door on the other side and watched the paintings watch us. The next room we entered was a kitchen. It was very large with a huge fire place that took up the whole wall. It had been modernized with four sets of stove tops on an island that ran though the middle of the room and along the wall were four built in ovens. A very large sink sat under a window. It was the kind of kitchen a chef would have dreamed of. We moved through another door into what appeared to be a mans sitting parlor. It had a pool table, fire place, a built in bar ,overstuffed chairs, couches, and large coffee tables made of thick wood. This room was made for a man, there was no doubt about that. The walls were aligned with all kinds of old books. Jim could not help himself and had to sit down in the large chair.

"You know what, Hun?, I could get used to coming home and relaxing here every day".
"Yeah, I bet you could."
" Why don't you like this old place? I think it would be kinda cool to live in a house like this. You know, we could call the movers today and be moved in by tomorrow".
 Standing there, I thought about what he had said to me. We could move in as it was larger then what we had now and this was probably my familys old homestead.
"Ok Jim, lets do it"!

I found myself saying it before my mind could think about it. What was I doing? I don't want to live here, I wanted to run from here screaming. Why had I said yes?

Looking over at Jim, he looked so  happy. That is why, I thought , love.


Chapter4

The warning

The next few days went by in such a blur it was like my life was spinning out of control. We had called the movers and they came and opened up the old house . It turned out the upper rooms where filled with the furniture from the house already, so we didn't need to move any into the house. We were packing up our clothing when   my parent's lawyer came by. He said he was just there to check up on us and see how we were doing. When we told him about the other house he went pale.

"Why didn't you and your husband call me when you found the papers?" he asked.
We just looked at each other puzzled.
"Well, we just thought you had forgotten to tell us about the house", my husband replied.
"No, I didn't. You are not to move into that house. It is cursed, that is why I never told you"!

I felt a chill run down my back. But Jim just laughed . The lawyer looked angry now At having been laughed at. I felt I should say something to ease the the mood in the room. "Why do people think the house is cursed"? He explained that a long time ago the house was owned by my family and back then it was a suger plantation. During the civil war the plantation was in full working order with over two hundred slaves. When the word went out that slavery was over, instead of freeing the slaves, my family decided to kill them all. He said that by morning the house and the grounds where covered in blood. Not one of the slaves made it away with their life. At hearing this, I had to sit down I felt so weak. The thought of my family being so cruel and heartless. left me was speechless. How could a person do that to another. I was trying to wrap my head around what he was saying to me when he told us that one of the slaves cursed the house , that for ever and all time, none of my blood line would be able to live there. That all who had tried had gone mad, killed themselves , or died terrible deaths. He walked over to me and took my hand.

"Please, I'm begging you, don't move into that house, it is evil, full of nothing but death!"

I looked up at him, and seeing his eyes, I could tell he was telling me the truth . My husband came over and put his arm around the back of my chair and rubbed my shoulder.

"We have already decided to move, no ghost is going to change that".

I looked up at Jim, so strong, so sure of everything in life. He was my rock that I leaned on.

"Sir, as my husband said, we are going there to live". Even hearing myself speak , I could hear the fear in my voice.

"Then I wish you all all the luck in the world ." He turned and walked toward the door, then as he was walking out, turned and looked right at me and said "and that you make

it out alive".




Chapter5

The people


The day we moved in was a beautiful day. The sun was shining, and the birds sang,

but me, I felt like I was moving into a grave. I felt sick at seeing the house again. The

people Jim had hired to fix up the place had done a good job. It looked wonderful, so

why was I feeling this way, like I was on my way to death row. I knew if I could just

make it through today it should be easier with time. So I tried to stay busy, which was

not hard as there was still so many things to get done. I was working in the kitchen

putting up some plates when a knock came from the screen door. I looked up to see a

woman looking back at me smiling.

"You must be the misses of the house . My name is Clara. I was sent by your family

lawyer to help you about the house".

" I don't understand, I didn't ask for him to send any help ".

"Well, I just go where I'm told, child, now where can I start".

" You don't understand, I don't have the money to hire help for the home".

"It was all taken care of, you see, when you moved in the house, you also get the money from the house Itself", she explained, "to run the house, it was part of the will and all".

" I never knew that, so you are paid by the lawyer?"

"Yes, misses".

" Well, I can't argue with that now can I?".

"Nope, O' yeah, there are others coming too. They will be working here, that's in the will as well".

" I guess, the more the merrier".

I finished putting up the dishes when I heard Jim outside the house yelling at someone. I went outside to see what was going on and when I turned the corner of the house, what I saw almost knocked me down. There were about fifty people clearing out all the brush from the back of the house. I came over to my husband and asked what was going on. He told me that the lawyer had sent these people to help clear the land and the will paid for it all. I explaind to him about the woman in the house.

"That explains the deal about the " haunted house" .

"What do you mean". I asked?

"Well", Jim explained "if your family had all this money and we could not get it until we moved into the house then the lawyer had it to begin with, which means if we had never found out about the house he could have kept it and we would have never known".

" Yeah, I guess it does make sense".

We just stood there and watched as the men worked cleaning the land, I could not help but wonder what other surprises would be happening.

Chapter 6

The life

That night, when we went to bed, it was late. Jim had called the lawyer and found out

that we were very well to do money wise, so much so, that Jim could quit the job he had

and stay home. The only hitch was that the plantation would have to put out sugar. So

Jim said to call him "sweetie" now cause that was our new life. It was going to be all

about the cane. That night I had trouble going to sleep I just thought it was because of

all the excitement of the day. I got up to get a drink of water when I heard a sound

coming from outside our bedroom door. I opened the door expecting to see someone,

 but there was no one  there, but there was a plastic red ball.  I picked the ball up

wondering where it had come from. We had no children , nor did we have any toys. I

put the ball back down in the hallway and made a mental note to talk to Jim about it in

the morning. And went back to bed. Morning came sooner then I thought it would. I

woke with the smell of breakfast cooking. I rolled over smiling to myself. Jim was

always so sweet to me. To think he was down there right now making me breakfast, I

just had to smile. I got up , showered , dressed and headed down stairs.  When I reached

the dining room I saw Jim sitting at the table. The table was covered in food.

" Jim, why did you make all this food".

"I didn't, they did", he pointed to the kitchen.

As I walked toward the door it opened up and three women came out carrying more plates of food." Who are you people and where did you come from?". The shorter of the three spoke. "We where hired to work in the house, misses".

"Hired by who". I asked. The plumper one spoke next, "it is all in the will ,misses".

I turned and looked at Jim but he only shrugged. After we ate the food that the women prepared for us I wanted to speak to Jim about all this. I explained to him that it all seemed very strange these all people were just moving into this house without interviews or anything. I didn't like it, but he just told me that I was being crazy and it was all in the will, like they had said . I told him we needed to call the lawyer and find out if we could see this will, but he didn't seem like he cared. So I asked him if he didn't think it was odd about the story and now all these black people were showing up to work here. He turned to me and said I was being racist. I told him "no" I was not, just that it was really weird and creepy but he didn't seem to care so I dropped it. That day I tried to work around the house but every time I would start to do something a woman would come in and tell me I should not worry about it, that that was what they were there for and would take the job from me. It left me feeling useless in my own house. By noon I was not just frustrated ,I was pissed off over it all, so I went outside and sat on the porch to collect my thoughts. It all felt wrong, being here and having all these people working here like it was time moving backward. I never thought of myself as being racist, but it was not the fact that they were black, it was the fact that they were working in a house where so many slaves where killed. I closed my eyes , feeling the sun on my body so warm and relaxing.

"Beautiful day".

My eyes flew open to see a man standing before me . He was tall with blond hair ,blue eyes, and looking at me like he knew me.

"Yes, it is", O' god ! it was the man I had seen before, but who was he?

" I came to work, but I can't seem to find anyone who can tell me where to start".

" Well, I'm the lady of the house and I don't even know where to start". He now was looking at me like I was crazy, so I acted fast.

"My husband, Jim, is in the back, in the field out there. You should go and talk to him. I'm sure he can help you."

" Thank you , I will".

He walked off. I just sat there thinking what in the hell is going on now. Something was not right around here and I was going to find out what it was. I got up and headed into the house. The first woman I found was a tall thin girl who looked about my age. I asked her if she could help me by telling all the house ladies to meet me in the dining room in about thirty minutes, that I wanted to talk to them all. She said she would and I headed to the study to look up all I could on the house itself. I looked through all the papers I could find but it was no help. Most were just bookkeeping on the field work being done at the time, how much the crop was selling for, and so forth. I left the study feeling more stressed out than before.

Chapter 7

The sickness

When I reached the dining room there was ten women waiting for me. I thanked them for meeting with me and told them that I wanted to be active in the work done in the house. This seemed to confuse them. I went on to explain that I didn't like people taking over what I was doing when I'm doing it and to please not take offence as all of this was all new to me. I enjoyed them helping but I wished that things were different. But as the will was binding , lets just work together. I asked if anyone had any questions for me. The younger woman I had spoken to earlier asked if I was feeling okay as I looked pale. I said I was fine but they wanted me to lay down for awhile. So not wanting to show my anger at being told to go to my room, I went with the young woman to my room to rest. When I reached the room my bed was already turned down so I climbed in and soon fell fast asleep. My dream was very strange. I was making love to a man it was so real that I believed it to be my husband until I opened my eyes and saw the blue eye man looking down at me . I tried to get away from him but the dream turned bad. I was fighting him off of me but he would not let me go. I woke up screaming to find the thin girl with me calming me down. I was covered in sweat. She told me I had become ill and had been in bed for three days, but now my fever had broken so I should be ok. I stared at her in disbelief. When I asked to see my husband she told me  to rest for now. I laid back and shut my eyes to rest. I was awakened to see the doctor sitting on my bed with my husband. I saw the concern on their  faces while they spoke too low for me to hear.

"What is wrong with me"? I asked.

" O thank God you're awake"! Jim said, smiling down at me.

" What is wrong with me"? I asked again.

The doctor looked at Jim ,then back at me.

" Well, your pregnant".

I could not think at that moment . A baby, now, everything going on. I looked at my husband sitting there , he looked so happy. A baby. Wow. The doctor went on to explain that I had gotten a flu of some kind and with me being pregnant and all the excitement of  the move, he believed that it all took its toll on me but the baby was still there and fine. I would have to come in and have some test done but all was normal from what he could tell. I was about two months along.

After the doctor left the room Jim filled me in on everything I had missed. It seemed the house was running fine without me . The workers had the field cleaned off and had started getting the ground ready for the crop to start going in the ground. He was beaming with the pride of a well satisfied man. I was happy for him . He loved the work and was glad that we had moved into the house. We talked about the baby. I expressed the fact that I was worried about having a baby so soon. He told me not to worry  about it. All would be fine as it always would be with us. The next few days were hard. The women had moved in the old slaves rooms on the upper floors and were running the house like bees' in a hive. I was weak and still had a low fever. They made me stay in bed a lot during the day, to build my strength up to give the mister a healthy baby , that is what they would tell me. Two weeks went by and I was feeling a lot better. My only problem was, I felt lonely. At night Jim would come in from the field too tired to talk to me . He would just shower ,eat and go to bed. I had tried to engage him in lovemaking but he was always too tired and if I pushed the subject he would get mad. He never got mad at me before we Moved here. The night was filled with odd sounds all the time. Footsteps where no one was, banging, laughter. One night I decided to talk to the women about it. I was thinking that some had men come to their rooms at night. I understand about all of the things between a man and a woman but they could at least keep the noise down. The next day I told them just that. A few blushed, others giggled. I myself just had to smile. What I had to smile about was the fact, here I was telling them to keep it down when I was the one pregnant. Yeah, funny. I had made friends with the older lady I had first met, Clara. She pretty much told everyone what to do, including me. She was like the mother I wish I had growing up. She told me she had nine kids, who had kids of their own. When I asked her how many, she just laughed and said "more then she could count." I found myself loving our chats together in the afternoon' sun on the porch. So much so, I confided in her my fears of what was going on in my life. The strange dreams I was having about the man, about the story the lawyer had told us and with them all showing up to work here. After I was done she just sat back in her rocking chair and smiled. Her only words were for me not to worry, she would take care of me and the baby.

Chapter 8

The nightmares


The night was not my friend in this house. The dreams got worse and Jim thought I

was going crazy. He had changed so much. The man I was going to bed with was not the

man I had married. He seemed much colder now, It had been three months now, and I

was starting to show a little. I had been going to the doctor with Clara because Jim told

me he was too busy to come with me . By now I was dreaming every night of the blond

man climbing into our bed and having violent sex with me. I could not tell Jim this in

fear he would think I was wanting to have this man in real life . That was what Clara

told me . That men think that way. I told her the man would rape me in my dreams but

she said all Jim would understand was that I was dreaming of another man so I remained

silent about the dreams. Until one night the dream was so bad it woke Jim up after

hearing me cry out. Instead of comforting me he was mad and told me that from now on

he was going to sleep in another room of the house. I begged him not to leave our bed,

that I was afraid to be alone. He looked at me and said to grow up. When I told him we

should leave, that it was the house. I thought he would hit me . He told me we would

never leave the house, not ever. He stormed out of the room leaving me to cry myself to sleep. The next morning I hurried down stairs to see him ,hoping to speak with him before he went to the field, but he was already gone. After I ate breakfast I went outside to help hang the laundry when I saw the man from my dreams coming from out of the barn. I could not think as my mind left me. All I could do was stand there and stare at him. Then I saw Jim come out of the barn as well, and he shook the man's hand . Jim saw me and frowned . He started to walk toward me, and I was begging myself in my head to look way, to move or to do something anything but stare.

"What are looking at Hun"? he asked.

"Who is that man Jim"? Even hearing my own voice I could hear the fear there.

"What's wrong with you, are you sick again"?

"No, I just don't like the looks of him. What does he want"?

"Well, he is working to fix up the barn's here. Woman, you get weirder every day, just go on in the house and get us something to drink".

"What ever happened to asking nicely".

"Just do it. Thanks to you, I could not sleep at all last night. It has put me behind in the field, so just do it, Now"!

I went in the house and made two glasses of tea , then headed toward the barn . With each step I was trying to build my courage up enough to face this man who raped me in my dreams. I could not let my fear show, I could not let anything show. Jim might get the wrong idea and think something was going on with this man. Before I knew it I was there entering the barn. But looking around I did not see anyone there. I just put the tea glasses down on a table and turned to leave when he stepped out of a stall.

"Hi, how are you doing"?

I just stood there unable to speak, afraid of what I might say.

"Hey, are you ok? You don't look good".

"Where is my husband"? I stammered.

"He went out back to get some nails, are you sure you're ok"?

He reached out for me, but I quickly jerked away.

" Don't touch me, don't ever touch me". I turned and ran for the door with him running

behind me, I opened the door and ran straight into my husband knocking him down.

"What the hell is going on here, what is wrong? Who are you running from"?

I turned to see the man looking at us.

"Him" I heard myself say.

"Why"? Jim asked . I just turned around and ran to the house, leaving them both behind

.

Chapter 9

The fall out


That night I made sure I locked my door, keeping my husband out and everyone else.

I didn't want to see anyone, not Jim, Clara, no one. Jim called the doctor. I told him to

go away too. But soon it became clear that was not going to happen. I had to let him in.

He took my blood pressure and said it was high, and I needed to stay in bed for awhile.

I agreed. Jim came in after the doctor had left and told me he had called Beth and she

said she would come and stay for a few days with us and take care of me. Then he

asked me what had happened in the barn. I told him nothing, I just didn't want to be

alone with that man. He asked if the man had touched me or done anything to frighten

me. I told him no, he got up to leave , I begged him to stay the night in our bed . He just

said for me to get some rest. That night the man came to me again in my dreams only

this time he was gentle with me and I felt myself willing to give in. If only to feel the

love of a man, if nothing else. That night I did give into the dream and I slept like I had

not in months.

When I woke up the next day the sun was just rising. I got up and went out onto the porch, just outside of my room. The air was a little cool it felt good on my skin. Then I saw him just below me, staring at me, watching me. It was him, the man from my dream and I could not help but blush. Then he smiled at me. I turned and quickly went back, in shutting the doors and locking them. I walked to my bedroom door opened it and peeked out into the hallway just in time to see the young thin woman leaving my husbands room. She was buttoning up her dress. I shut my door  and she didn't see me. I heard her walk past my room and head down the stairs. All I could think about  was, damn him.

Damn him to hell! I waited in my room until I was sure he was gone from the house then I made my way down to eat breakfast.  I thought as I ate of what to do about all of this. I loved Jim, he loved me. Why would he do this? Was it a moment of weakness? Was it because of  the baby? Why? I had to find Clara and tell her about it . Yes, Clara would know what I should do. I got up and went looking for her. It took only a few moments before I found her cleaning the upper floor rooms. I took her outside and told her all about what I had seen. Then asked what should I do.

"You should kill him". she said

I looked at her in disbelief.

"What"?

"I would if it was me", she said. And with that, she just got up and walked off. I just sat there. How could she have said that to me. I needed her and she said that to me. I could not kill Jim , I love him. Didn't I?

That night I waited to talk to him. I told him all about what I had seen. He told me it was my fault, that I caused him to do it. He said  I was going crazy and that he had needs. If I could not give him what he wanted, he would get it from someone else. I told him the same was for me, that I would get it from some one else too. That was when it happened. He hit me. I had never been hit by a man before, let alone Jim. I fell to the floor, stunned. Then the pain came. It started in my back and went around the front. Jim was still standing over me, cursing me, when I saw the blood begin to form on the floor under my dress. He saw it to. And all he could do was yell for help as I laid there and lost our baby. Death had come to me again, not to take my life but my child's life. By the time the doctor had come and gone I was unable to feel anything. I felt no pain, sorrow, or hate. I was numb. Jim had lied and said I fell down the stairs. I said nothing, I didn't care what was told except that I wished I could die. That night Beth arrived and spent the night sleeping in a chair beside my bed. She tried to talk to me but I would not talk. I could not make my mouth form any words to say anything. I was living but I felt dead all the same. That night all I dreamed of was blackness, being surrounded by it, reaching out to it only for it to slip away. I spent the next month in bed without speaking. I just had nothing to say. It was that day I heard the voice for the first time. Soft, like a whisper at first, for me to open my eyes and look at him. When I did, I saw the man from my dreams standing in my room. I was frightened, and I pulled the cover up to my chin. Looking around I saw Beth, and Clara too. Beth reached out and took my hand.

"Honey, we need to talk to you, can you understand what I'm saying to you"?

I nodded my head for yes.

" Baby, there was an accident this morning out in the field. Do you understand me"?

I nodded.

"Baby, Jim was hurt, "and she started to cry.

Clara spoke up then.

"Jim is dead".

I just sat there, looking at them. He was dead. Jim, my Jim, dead. No, this could not be happening! My baby, then my husband. Dead. But not me. Why not me? I felt the darkness closing in on me, then, nothing. I was floating in darkness. In the darkness I prayed for death, but it would not come. It just would not come.

Chapter 10

The dawn


I was told it had been a week before I fully came out of the sleep. The doctor had

been by every day to check on me. He told Beth it was from grief. He was right. I felt

I had nothing to live for anymore. This house had taken its toll on me. I just had to get

away for a while. So, I went to the house of my parents only to find out it had been sold

by Jim. I was now lost. I went back to the big house only to find out that Clara was

waiting for me. She said that Beth had gone to run some errands and would be home

soon. She begged me to eat something, so I did. But the food had no taste in my mouth.

 I felt as if I was going to go crazy. I was now trapped here alone in this house. The

house was slowly killing me just like I was told it would. I got up from the table and

went out on the porch to wait for Beth to come back. It soon was starting to get dark.

The wind was picking up and it was growing colder. I walked inside to get warm when I

saw a little girl standing in the dining room. She looked lost. I asked her where her

mother was but she just giggled and ran off toward the kitchen. I followed her only to

find that she was no longer in there. Instead Clara was. When I asked about the little girl

she told me she had not seen her. Puzzled, I walked out the back door to see if she was

In the yard, but no one was there. As I walked in some of the other women were now in the kitchen. They watched me as if I was crazy. I felt crazy. I guess it showed. Clara was the one who spoke first.

"Misses, we would like to have tomorrow off, if we could".
I said the only thing I could think of.
"Yes, you can. Will everyone be taking the day, even the men in the field"? I asked.
"yes". Clara said.
" Fine ," I said and walked out of the room. Leaving them to talk about me behind my back like I knew they would.

I made my way up the stairs to my room to go to bed. The sheets were fresh. I Needed that tonight. The smell of happiness, fresh sheets. Soon I was fast asleep, only to be awakened by the sound of screaming. I awoke not in my bed but standing in my room. I ran to the door jerking it open to find a woman's body lying outside of it. She was dead. Then I heard more screaming. The house seemed to be alive with the screams of people and, then I smelled the smoke. I ran down the hallway. There was blood and bodies laying everywhere. Women and men. I ran as fast as I could down stairs, feeling the heat from the fire all around me. I ran out the front door. I looked down at my body to see myself covered in blood. In front of me the house loomed in flames like some kind of monster. Filled with the screams of the dying and the lost. Then I felt things in each of my hands. Looking down I saw a lighter, in the other hand was a gun. There was blood on me. What had I done! O' God ,what had I done! I felt my body jerk. Then another jerk. I looked down and saw two holes in my chest. Turning, I saw a cop yelling for me to drop the gun. I did as I fell to the ground. The darkness was closing in on me now. I welcomed it.

Reached for it and embraced it.

You see, this is a ghost story after all.

 My ghost story.

2.My madness chapter 11- 20

Chapter11

Monday


I remember the day like it was yesterday. I woke up that morning and got ready for

school. Starting the eleventh grade was going to be hard. I had barely made it though

tenth. Anyway, I got down stairs and grabbed a glass of o j on my way out. My mom

was yelling at me to eat but , hey, I was late anyway. The bus left without me  so I was

running, trying to get there before the first bell rang. I was about a block from the school

when it appended. The next thing I knew I was waking up in the hospital with my mom

and dad crying beside me. The next few days drug on like a bad dream. They said I was

lucky to be alive. The car that hit me had lost control due to the brake pads not being

changed. I didn't feel all that lucky with a  broken leg, broken pelvic bone, and some

head trauma. I guess I should be glad I'm alive, right? Wrong. That was the day I started

hearing "them." They would call to me from down the hall of the hospital. At first I

though it was the guys from school playing some kind of  trick, until I realized that the

people I was hearing were dead.

I left the hospital about a week after I got there. Man, Mom and dad were so mad at

me they would not even speak to me. Which was fine really, 'cause all they would have

done was yell anyway. We got home and I headed up to my room, with a little help from them of course. So I spent a few months in bed and it really sucked! Now I should say right now that the dead are not good people to hang out with. Now, you're probably asking yourself questions like: were you not upset that dead people were talking to you? Or are you sure you didn't hit your head harder then what the doctor thought? Yea, I know. But I have always liked the whole "life after death" though myself so I dealt. But nothing could have prepared me for what would happen the day I finely went to school.

Chapter12

School


When I got to school it was all a buss, like it always is. Kids  running to class, trying

not to be late but still trying to get some hall time in . I found some of my guys I hung

out with talking on the way to class. First I had gym which was cool, I could sleep. I had

just laid down on the bleachers outside on the track field when I felt a cold chill run

through me. I opened my eyes and looked to my left, and across the field I saw a woman

walking. She had blood on the front of what looked like a nightgown. I quickly look the

other way, not wanting her to know I saw her. I was trying to make up my mind if she

was alive or dead when my answer came with the touch of her hand on my arm, ice

cold. Yep, she was a deader. I tried to act like I could not feel it but it was kind of like

dumping a bowl of cold jelly over your arm and not reacting. I turned toward her.

"Am I dead?" she asked me.

"Yes, I think that you are. What is your name?"

"I don't know."


Then , just like that , poof, she was gone. I have to admit that this was the first time I

had one of the "living impaired" ask me if they were dead or not. I sat and pondered the thought. Most did not know that they were dead and that is why they were ghosts. This one though, she knew she was, so, why was she still here on earth? I was still thinking it over when a buddy of mine came over to chat me up.

"Hey man, great to see you here in one piece."
"Yea man, glad to be here".

We chatted until the bell rang . Nothing too heavy, just stuff, but I could not get the Woman out of my mind. You know, looking back on it, I wished I would have just forgotten all about it then and there, but I can't ever seem to let sleeping dogs lie. That afternoon when I got home I ran upstairs and got online and tried to find out anything I could about the Woman, but as big as the web is, unless you got a name or something, it is almost impossible. Not impossible, just almost. I knew she was dead so I started looking for anyone that had died within the past few weeks. I came across a story in the paper about a house fire and a woman shot by the police. I sat back in wonder. It was her in the picture. Oh, wow! Was all I could think. This woman had killed a house full of people before she was shot by police. I turned off my pc and went down to eat and try to forget what I had read. My mom's cooking was good but still, I had a bad taste in my mouth when I went to bed that night. It was like I knew that I had  stepped into something big and I didn't want to be in it at all. Lying in bed that night all I could think of is, why? Why did she do it? And how could I help her "move on." I closed my eyes with her name on my lips. "Hope". Her name was Hope.

Chapter 13

The night


I was in the dark. Something was moving around me. I reached out and felt
something cold and metal. I picked it up, it felt like a flash light. I turned it on. I was
standing in a grave yard. My mind went into overload. What the hell was I doing here?
What is going on? How did I get here? I shine4d the flash light over the head stone:


Beloved Wife

Hope Ann Berry

June 2, 1985- October 20, 2004


All I could think about at this point was I need to get the hell out of here, NOW!
I ran like I have never ran before through the trees on the back side of the grave yard . I
turned down a dirt road and did not stop running until I reached the back side of the
school. Then, I just stopped. In front of me, standing there , was her.

" Why are you running from me?"

I thought real hard for a few seconds before I answered.

"Why are you stalking me? You know that is a crime". Man, what a stupid thing to say, I know, I know, but I did. She only laughed at me, making the hair rise on the back of my neck. Then she walked toward me. Now, I would like to tell you I stood there cause I'm cool and brave....nah. .I was scared shitless.. could not move at all, completely frozen to the spot. Then she spoke to me again.

"I like you, your sweet".

"No I'm not. You don't even know me. I'm mean, I'm bad and evil". Yes, I was ready to crap myself at this point. Not only was I making a fool out of myself by what I was saying but she was now laughing at me. I thought about it for a moment and got up the guts I knew I had somewhere stashed and opened my big fat mouth.

" I didn't know ghosts could laugh". At hearing ghost she stopped and glared at me.

" I need your help". she said.

"No, you don't. you need to move on to the next life".

"But I can't without your help."

"Forget it, you're on you're own lady". I turned to walk away when it happened. I felt a sharp pain in my arm. Turning, I saw her hand on me. My god! She could touch me! Like a real person. Now is the point in the story I am not proud of. I screamed like a seven year old girl and passed out. I mean flat out. Even thought I had passed out, I felt like I was flying. Like I was light as a feather, floating in a breeze. Then nothing. Just sleep.

Chapter 14

The day


I awoke with a start. Jumping out of the bed and looking around the room. It was

all a dream. Damn! What a dream. I had to sit down on the bed and collect myself. What

the hell was happening to me? Was I going crazy? I had to fix whatever was going on

with the chick and myself 'cause if I didn't I would end up in a padded room with a

matching coat , the kind that buttons in the back. I did the only thing I could think of . I

skipped school and went to the library to do some reading. Now, I should say right off

the bat that me and the library are not friendly. I don't like it , it don't like me. I can't

find anything there nor do I care to. If I need a paper wrote for class I pay someone to do

it for me. Well, today I thought, "I'm was on my own." I went though a lot of papers.

Mostly about the town and the house she died at. Man, her family was messed up to say

it mildly. They owned slaves back in the day. When they could not anymore they killed

them. They also seemed to die a lot in that house. I found everything from murder to

heart attack. Some though were more simple then others to recall. Like the death of

someone being shot or stabbed. It seemed the house really was jinxed or something.

The only thing was that it was worth some meager cash. I found where her family was

all dead except for her and what seemed to be a cousin. He was listed as living in the next town over from us. I wrote the name and address down . I could try and call him, never know, he might talk to me. As long as I left out the Whole "I talk to the dead thing." I tried to find something on her husband but I could not. I thought that was odd but "o' well." I was starting to feel a little like I was in a tomb so I left the library to go by where the house was, or what was left of it.

When I got to the spot I was feeling like I was butting in where I should not be. There was a girl standing looking at what was left of the house. I watched her for a moment before walking up to her.

"Hi" I said quietly "did you know someone who lived here". she nodded.

"Yeah, my grandmother. She was working here when the fire broke out, she didn't make it".

"I'm sorry to here that". Now I just felt sick. I wanted to ask some more questions but felt like a real ass for even thinking it. I was so glad that she made the first move and asked me some questions.

"Did you lose someone to"?

"No,".

"I want to find out what happened", she said and looked at me.

"Well, I kind of do to, but more for my own mind."

She smiled at me. The kind of smile that made me feel really good inside. Until she opened her mouth, that is.

"So are you, like, one of those guys that love death and destruction or are you just morbid?"

That stunned me for a second but I recover quickly from anything.

"No, I just got a curious kind of mind is all. I did a little look up on this place and found out that a lot of people have died here and I was wondering what it all was about."
"Really? Well, my grandmother was not to happy to work here, I know that. She called and said that the misses of the house was losing her mind. So much so that her husband left her after she lost her baby. Not only that but they told her he died, they were worried she might kill herself if she knew the truth. "
"Looks like that was a bad idea". I said thinking about all of it." that might be what sent her over the edge".
She looked down at the ground.
" I think it was."
We stood there for a while not speaking, just, being.
"By the way, my name is Jane".
"Oh, well mine is David."

Chapter 15

My new friend

We talked for a while. Me and Jane. We also compared notes of what we knew. I just

left out the ghost thing. I have not told anyone about that yet. She gave me her number

and I gave her mine. When I got home mom was waiting to chew me up and spit me out

over skipping school. But when I told her I went to the library I thought she was going

to pass out. To make it worse was when I asked where the phone was so I could call

Jane. Well, my mom is just a little bit of a drama queen. She was so happy I was calling

a girl she didn't even ground me for skipping. We talked on the phone until late in the

night. It was cool to find someone to talk to. She was a year younger then me and way

out of my league. Still, I could see something coming of all of this. That night I took

some sleeping pills so I would not dream. It was cool that it worked. I woke up nice and

refreshed. I head off to school with a newfound love of the place. My first class went

smoothly without a ghost showing up. My next class was the best. I was just sitting

There trying not to fall asleep when I got the shock of my life. Jane walked into the

room. It was like a breath of fresh air had entered my life. I knew that this was going

to be a great year after all. She had gotten her parents to transfer her to my school.

Seemed they were glad she had met someone too. We had lunch together and I walked her home. We stood outside her house talking for a while then said our good byes and I headed home. Only I didn't get too far until I saw the ghost woman again. Now I'd like to point out that, again, Ghosts don't scare me, but, and this is a big but, this one "Hope" scares the hell out of me. I tried to keep walking and prayed that she would not see me and would keep going wherever it was she was heading. Well, my luck is not so good. She followed me about two blocks, then, just appeared in front of me.

"I'm prettier then her".

I just stood there in shock. She's been watching me, all day!

" Don't you think I'm prettier then her?"

This is just too far out there for my mind to relate to. I thought quickly for the right thing to say, then opened my mouth.

"Well, you are pretty, but she is alive and you're dead." Now is the part where I point out that I am not too smart, just in case your reading this and it has not crossed your mind already. She did not like that answer a bit more then anyone would, let alone a crazy ghost. She smiled at me and then said the one thing that chilled me to the bone.

"I could help her with that. The whole living thing is so over rated".

Now I was pissed.

"You stay the hell away from her! She has nothing to do with what happened to you. I don't either for that matter. Go haunt someone else and leave me the hell alone!"

"So, you like her." she giggled. It was a sound I never hoped to here again. Then she stopped and glared at me.

"Help me and she lives. Don't, and she will die."

My mind went blank. My blood ran cold. I shook allover with anger. But before I could

calm down I open my month again.

" You crazy bitch! No wonder your husband left you!"

I knew when I said it that I should have kept quiet. The look of rage flooded her face

and she screeched at me.

" My husband is dead! He loved me! It was that whore that was taking him away from

me!

He got what was coming to him! He is dead!"

I took a deep breath. I had to tell her the truth that I knew so far.

"He is alive," I when on, "He left you because he thought you where loosing your mind.

He was right, you killed all those people."

"They deserved to die. They were leaving me, everyone leaves me."

Then poof, she was gone again.

Chapter 16

The search

The next day I talked to Jane about the missing husband. She told me he had move

across town . We looked him up online and went to his home. When he answered the

door I have to admit he looked like shit and smelled like he had took a bath in some kind

of beer. When we told him why we were there he tried to shut the door in our faces but

he was too drunk and ended up falling over. I helped him back inside the house and

onto the couch. I sent Jane to find the kitchen and make some coffee so we could talk

alone. I asked him about Hope. He looked up at me and burst into tears. I just sat there

holding this drunken, crying man, feeling like I had truly hit rock bottom. After a few

minutes of this he seemed to pull himself together enough to tell me that he had to leave

her for her own good. He said she thought he was cheating on her with one of the

women that worked at the house. I asked the question why she would think that . He

replied that she claimed to have seen the woman coming out of his room, buttoning up

her dress. He also claimed that he never touched the woman but his wife had the nerve

to think it so he did not deny it to her. I thought yep, that's a man for you. Always

wanting to think all women wanted him. Made me glad I was not like that. I had no ego.

Didn't want one either. Then he told me that his friend Devin was the one that told him he should leave. That name rang a bell in my head. I knew I had heard the name before but I wasn't sure where. When I asked why his friend would want him to leave his wife he told me that she had made a move on his friend. That took me aback some. Everything I had learned about Hope so far did not fit with her being a run-a-bout. I was just about to ask about this Devin guy when Jane came in with the coffee. I have to say I was glad to see her. I got up and let her sit next to the guy . I really didn't want to be cried on anymore. I sat across from him and asked the big question. Who was Devin? He told me the guy came to work for them after they moved into the house. He helped with fixing the barns and in the field some. It seemed like he really knew his way around the place. He went on about the guy like he was a saint. When I asked about where he was now I was told he didn't know. Feeling like I had gotten all I could for now we said our good byes and left. We were on our way over to my house when I saw Hope peeking out from behind a tree. I tried not to show my fear when Jane stopped walking and grabbed my arm.

"What's wrong?"
"What do you mean"? I tried to shrug it all off.
"You look like you just saw a ghost". she laughed. God, if she only knew!
"Yeah, right. Nah, just a little worried about you meeting my folks. My mom might start planning the wedding".

That was when it happened. I felt the coldness of Hopes arms around me, looking down At my chest, I saw she had wrapped her arms around me. Oh, God, not now! Then darkness.

Chapter 17

Life is strange

I woke up in a hospital bed. The bad news was I was in a hospital bed. The good news was that Jane was laying on the bed with me asleep. Now, I have to admit I am a guy all for waking up with a girl on the bed with me . Well, that truly rocks! Until I looked over to see my mom sitting in the chair in front of the bed. Total buzz kill. I moved my arm, waking Jane up.

"Hey sleepy head". I said smiling. She gave me a sleepy smile back but when she saw mom she almost feel of the bed. I had to grab her to keep her on.

"O, God, I'm so sorry. I was sleepy , I just fell asleep. I didn't want to leave you and your mom was not here yet and , I was on top".

I could not resist. She was so embarrassed.

" I can see you were on top. It's cool".

"No! I mean I was on top of the cover".

" Yeah, I know".

" Oh , man".


We looked over at my mom. Bless her heart. She just sat there with this smile on her face. Probably counting the grandkids in her head. Jane moved off the bed. Then the though came back to me of where I was.

"Why am I in the hospital?"

My mom came over to us.

"Well, you passed out and this fine young woman had the right mind to call an ambulance to come and get you".

I looked at Jane.

"Really?" I asked. She just blushed.

"I was worried when you just fell over. You really scared me". she then pinched me on the arm.

"Ouch, what was that for?"

"For scaring me. Don't do it ever again, ok"?

God, I was starting to love this girl.

"I'll try not to".

"Now", mom asked, "what happened"?


We looked at each other and told mom the whole story. After we were done we waited for her to speak, thinking she would blow her top or tell us not to see each other again. Instead she hugged us both. She told us she herself love a good mystery and to be sure to tell her how it all ends, just that we better not get into any trouble along the way.

We all sat and talked for awhile until then the doctor told me I could leave so I did. We dropped Jane off at her house and headed home. When we got there I ran up to my room just to chill for awhile. Boy, that was a bust when I opened my door and saw Hope sitting on my bed. I said the first thing that came to my mind.

"You keep the hell away from me, you crazy bitch! Don't you ever fucken touch me again!"

"Oh, but David, you love me, don't you. I make your life worth living".

Then she was at my side saying:

"I could take this away just as easy ,you know. I could take her away."

"Leave her out of this. It is between you and me, not her!"

" I know where you were because, I saw him. My husband." then she did the sick laugh again. I was about to really go off on her when I heard door bell ring. That made her giggle with delight.

"They are here for you now, David", she giggled. I heard my mom yell for me to come down stairs.

"Who is here?" I was freaking out now.

"The cops", she giggled louder." You see, you killed my husband.

I stared in disbelief as she disappeared. All I could think was " oh shit"!

Chapter 18

You got nerve

I'm looking around the room and wondering weather I should  go down or out the window. If I ran they would pin it on me for sure, or even worse on Jane. My mom opened the door of my room before I had made my mind up. Behind her were two cops looking like they came straight out of law and order.

"Honey, these nice police officers want to talk to you about where you were today". I could not help but think that she would not still call them nice after they beat me with a rubber hose or what ever it was they do to get you to confess to something when you didn't do it. "Ok." was all I said.

They asked me a lot of questions, about why I was there ,who I was with , if it could be verified ,and all that stuff. I told them what we had told mom earlier . They told me that they believed me. I was so happy I almost hugged them. Me and mom walked them to the door in time to see Dad pull up. So I had to explain it all to him that night. When I went to bed that night I decided to tell Jane about the ghost thing. I felt bad not telling her about what danger being around me could bring her. I prayed for a good nights sleep before drifting off to the dream world. The next day I met her at school . We went out on the track to talk. Then I dropped the bomb.

" You can see dead people!'

"Yes".

"Like real dead people".

"yes".

"Talk to them and they talk back, these dead people".

"Yes!"

"Cool". I just looked at her and stopped walking.

"Cool?"

She looked at me.

"Yeah, cool". and kept on walking.

"Oh, hold on there. I just told you the most craziest thing in the world and you say cool?"

She stopped.

"Seeing a ghost is not the most craziest thing in the world." she thought for a moment," telling me you're from another planet would be, you're not are you?"

"No,  I just see ghosts."

"Well, ok then". she kept on walking. Then I guess it finally got to her what I was really trying to say, because she turned white.

"You can see her, can't you? That's what happened that day you passed out. You saw her. Oh, god. She found him because of us and killed him, didn't she?"

I just nodded. Now she looked sick. She sat down on the ground. Damn, I hope she doesn't pass out now was all I could think. Then I knew I could not tell her about the threat on her. I knew I could protect her after all, there was no reason to get her more upset. I sat down beside her and just held her thinking, yeah, I love this girl. She looked up at me after a while and said the words I had been wanting to here from the day I first saw her.

"David, I think I'm falling in love with you."
I smiled at her.
"yeah , I think I'm already in love with you". we were just about to kiss when we heard what sounded like a bomb going off. Turning, we saw a car in the student parking lot in flames. Jane jumped up and took off running I followed her yelling for her to stop. She did once she reached the fence sounding the track.
"No!" she was screaming.
"What is it. Do you know the car?"
"Yes! Yes! She looked at me with fear in her eyes. It's mine!"

Chapter 19

Playing it cool

After the fire trucks had left the cops had a lot of questions for the two of us. From what they had found so far the car had just exploded on its own, for no reason, just went boom. They told Jane she was lucky to be alive because if she would have been in it she would not be here. After all the questions were done the principle sent the both of us home. The Problem was, we didn't want to go home. Instead, we went to the library to chat a little and do some research. We had gotten though the first hour before she asked the one question I was not ready to answer.

"She wants me dead, don't she"?

"Well", I said " not really. She wants me to help her and she thinks you're in the way of me doing that".

"So when were you going to tell me this".

" I was hoping not to have to tell you about it, but she has not given me the choice to do that, now has she"?

"Why does she want me dead anyway"?

"I think she is stalking me". At hearing this she turned from her book with a grin on her face.

"You mean to tell me she has a crush on you?"

"Yeah, why do you think that's funny. I don't. She's crazy".

"Well, what are you going to do about it"?

I though for a moment. What am I going to do? I mean, it is not like I can take out an order of protection or anything on her. Then it hit me.

"I'm going to do what she wants".

"What, you can't".

"Why not. If it saves you, I will".

She looked down at the stacks of books we were going through ,then back at me.

"Just tell me the plan".

I explained that she needed to know what happened to her. We had to find out about what caused her to go all nutty, then she would move on and leave us alone. We had a plan now. Only problem was getting it done. We had to find this Devin guy. I knew the name rang a bell but where from. Then it hit me, the cousin. I told Jane about it and we got to work finding all we could out about him. We even learned that him and the lawyer had the same address. Talk about weird. We barrowed my mom's car and headed to the house .When we got there  we watched the house for a short time until the door opened and a blond haired guy came out. From what I was told I believed it was Devin. He was followed by a slender guy with round glasses that I took to be the lawyer.  We were getting out of the car when we both got a shock. The two guys kissed each other. Now, I'm not homophobic or anything, but I have never seen it before . I was staring. I'm ashamed, but I was. In  my own defense, Jane was too.  We walked up to the couple, they were still embracing each other so  didn't notice until I said "excuse us." Then they quickly seemed to put a distance between each other. I explained I was from the paper doing a story on the house that burned and had learned that the man was kin to the woman. Jane was my photographer . We had the story down pat and preformed it to a tee, so much so they they I invited us in to talk. Boy ,did we learn a lot! It seemed that the cousin now owned the property and all that went with it. I was trying to decide on how to approach the question about him working there when the phone rang.  He excused Himself and answered it in another room. I took this time to talk to the lawyer about Hope. He told me the girl was troubled from the beginning. He warned her not to move into the house but she didn't heed his warning. When Devin came back into the room he was upset over something and I had a feeling I knew why.  He knew we where a fake. We needed to leave . Now. I said I was glad to meet them and we could show ourselves out. When he moved to block the door I knew I was right. We were told the usual stuff…"Your not going nowhere" and "Who sent you"? I played it cool though.  I told him to kiss my ass , kicked him in the balls, grabbed Jane's hand , and ran like hell out the door to the car and  left as fast has my mom's little Honda could go.

Chapter 20

The chat

I didn't let off the gas until we reached our own town. Jane loved it. Said I was her

hero. I said, " hell no" I was scared to the point of shitting myself ,but she just laughed.

Have I said before I loved this girl? We went to my house to hide out and eat some junk

food. I was not expecting to find Hope there in my room. Jane knew something was up

when I put myself in front of her.

"What do you want Hope"? I felt Jane grip my shirt from behind. Hope just smiled.

"I want you. To help me."

"I'm trying to help you, but you can't keep trying to hurt us".

"You want me to stop, tell me what I need to know".

So I did. I told her everything I had learned so far. Watching her face as I told her

was horrible. By this point, all joking put aside, I knew she was truly insane. Only now

she was pissed off too. She shot out of the room like a gust of cold air. she was gone.

Later that night we saw on the news that both Devin and the lawyer where dead. It

seemed they killed each other over the money from the will Devin had just received.

With it all being over you would think that my story ends here right. Wrong. Even though we helped her she still stalked me and Jane both. She even started stalking other people in the town. The longer she did it, the more and more people started to believe the whole town was haunted. They have even done a piece for it in the paper and on the six o'clock news. We never told anyone about her. Not until now that is. So, you might be asking your self, Why now? After all this time, why would I tell the story now? Simple . I believe the time has come to tell the story. You see, after me and Jane were married we settled down in a little house . The white picket fence, the whole nine yards. We lived happily until the day came when Hope returned into our lives. Only this time we where not ready for her. It was late at night, I had just kissed my twin girls good night when I saw her walking down the stairs. I thought it was my mind playing tricks on me until I reached the bottom of the stairs and saw her there, with Jane. I stayed calm and told Jane to go get the girls and leave the house. She just looked at me funny , and she asked me why and I mouthed the word "Hope". She left the room and pretty soon I hear the door shut and the car leave. Now came the time I had been dreading. Dealing with Hope.

"Why are you here Hope? We did what you wanted. Leave me and my family alone."
"You have blood on your hands too, David. You knew what I would do when you found them, still you gave them up. Why is that?"
"I thought it would make you cross over if you got your revenge on the ones that wronged you. Guess I was wrong."
"Yes, you see I still want you David. I will have you".
":No, I love my wife, move on Hope, to the other side . Heal yourself there."

"Not without you!"

That was when it happened. She lunged at me. Even though she was a ghost I still reacted like I would with it being any other person. The problem was that there was a brick fire place behind me with a fire poker, sharp side up, sticking out of its basket. I felt it as it entered my body. Looking down at it, all I could think was "damn."

So you see. This is not just her story. It is mine too.

My ghost story.

www.ingramcontent.com/pod-product-compliance
Lightning Source LLC
Chambersburg PA
CBHW020651130626
46552CB00003B/1496